OUT OF THE WOODS

BOOKS BY CLARK

THE STAINS OF TIME

The Piano of Death

The Boot of Destiny

The Chains of Desire

The Elixir of Denial

The Dance of Dreams

OTHER BOOKS

Those Little Bastards

All He Left Behind

Missing Mr. Wingfield

The Seven Wives of Silver

Bad Poetry Night

Out of the Woods

Under the World

OUT OF THE WOODS

E. CHRISTOPHER CLARK

Published in the United States by Clarkwoods in Chelmsford, Massachusetts.

ISBN for the Print Edition: 978-1-952044-08-3
ISBN for the Digital Edition: 978-1-952044-09-0
Library of Congress Control Number: 2018900405

CONTENTS

For my daughters, Kaylee & Melody; and for my wife, Stephanie, as always

ANYTHING BUT PURE

"There have been worse winters," his grandfather told him, as they stood between snowbanks that towered above him, that rose as high as Grandpa's chin in some places.

He couldn't picture it, and he told Grandpa as much. So, the old man put a hand on the boy's shoulder and told him to close his eyes.

The snow was only ankle-deep, Grandpa told him, but it was never the snow alone that made a winter bad. What made a winter bad was what the snow covered, what it sought to hide and to bury.

"Picture it," said Grandpa, "snow atop crumbling brick and burnt timber, atop family portraits and toy trains and baby dolls whose pretty dresses were soiled now with soot and worse."

The boy began to cry, but Grandpa didn't stop. It was no use denying the tears, he told the boy. Nothing wrong with crying, even when you were a man, when the memory called for it.

"Picture it," said Grandpa. "Picture what the snow was trying to hide from us as we stood there, looking at what our fighting had done. What a travesty it would have been," said Grandpa, "if we had forgotten what lay beneath that blanket of white, if we had succumbed to the Devil's call to see purity where there was anything but."

ONE PLAYER OR TWO?

I t was here. Fifteen minutes ago, it was here on the desk, next to the controller, beside the N.E.S. There was only the one and he's sure it isn't one of the coins in his hand because all he sees there is silver. No gold.

But wait, he thinks, pennies aren't gold. Even freshly minted, they aren't. They're copper, right? Copper.

Where is it? He checks under the rug again, inside his shoes one more time.

If the clerk at the Mickey Dee's was reasonable, it wouldn't matter. But the girl who works the Sunday night shift is a meth head, complete with missing teeth and runny nostrils and delusions of grandeur. For her, a penny is a penny is a penny.

On screen, the game he set up to simulate while he was gone is finished. He thinks to pause his quest, find the notebook, and take down the stats, but his stomach roars its disapproval and he keeps on keeping on.

Someone knocks at the door, one of his housemates, probably the ski bum who's offered him the ride, but maybe the ski bum's pigtailed girlfriend instead. It doesn't matter. He doesn't know either of their names, doesn't know the name of anyone in the house, and how can he ask for a penny without at least being able to ask them by name? "Hey You, could you give me a loan?" No, that won't fly. It has to be "Hey, Kurt" or "Yo, Tori" or else nothing at all.

"You almost ready?" It's the girl. Liz? Kim? Courtney?

"Almost," he says. "Just scrounging up some change."

"We can loan you some money, Evan."

Evan. Great. She knows his name. And what was that, the bit about scrounging up change? That was as good as asking, wasn't it? *What would Dad think?* asks the meanest of the voices in his head.

Dad's dead, he whispers to himself.

"What?" asks the girl on the other side of the door.

⚜

As they ride in Victor's car — Victor, the ski bum is called Victor — Tammy, the girl, asks him what's the deal with the video game.

"It's baseball," she says. "I get that. But what are you writing down in the notebook?"

"Stats," says Evan.

"The game doesn't do that for you?" says Tammy.

"Not really," he says. "Not in any meaningful way."

In the driver's seat, Victor chuckles. He makes the turn into the McDonald's parking lot.

"What's funny?" says Tammy.

Victor holds up a hand and shakes his head, staying silent.

It was Dad's thing, the stats. A long time ago, when they first got the game, they actually played it, actually sat down on opposite ends of the green and brown couch, controllers in hand, and took each other on. Dad mastered the pitching mechanic, Evan was unmatched in the virtual batter's box, and Mom, when she played, had a knack for the outfield that brought deep ball players to their knees. They had a blast. But once Dad found the "season" mode and realized you could simulate games in about a quarter of the time it took to play them, he got it into his head that he was going to see how things played out over the careers of their pixelated players, over the lifetimes of franchises not named for their real life counterparts, so as to avoid lawsuits from a league that hadn't quite figured out what to do with video games yet. He brought the original Nintendo to his office and bought a new Super Nintendo for Evan and Mom to play with in the living room.

"We all getting the same thing?" asks Victor, braking just shy of the Drive Thru.

"One patty melt," says Evan, handing his change up front.

Victor tosses the change into one of his cup holders, where it mingles with the quarters he keeps there for the tolls he pays to go home on weekends — he lives in Vermont; that much, Evan does remember. Victor holds out his hand to Tammy. From her purse, she produces a crisp twenty, depositing it into his palm.

Victor pulls forward, then orders.

✺

THE PATTY MELT is a thin slice of hamburger, covered in Cheese Whiz and diced onions, on a soggy rye bun. There is nothing appetizing about it, and Tammy and Victor are saying as much. They can't understand why Evan was so anxious to get one.

"Because they're only here for a limited time," says Evan, parroting the commercial he hears five times an afternoon while tucked away in his dorm room between the end of classes and the start of dinner. "You never know when they might be gone for good."

"Not a minute too soon," says Victor, dabbing at his lips with the wrapper, then tossing it out the window.

"Victor!" says Tammy, slapping at his arm.

"I couldn't stand the smell," he says. "You should get rid of yours, too."

"I will," she says, "in a trash can, when we get home."

Victor adjusts his rear view, as if to look Evan in the eye by way of the mirror. "Is this another of those family traditions?" he asks. "Did you and your father go out for shitty fast food every Sunday?"

Tammy hits him again, this time with a closed fist instead of an open palm. She knows — they both know, apparently — how much Evan is missing his father.

"Only when there was something new on the menu," says Evan. "Like, last year, when BK had their Italian chicken sandwich," he says, though that was one he had more often with the girlfriend who worked at the Dunkin Donuts across the street, the sandwich it had felt weird to eat with Dad, because of the things he and the Dunks girl had done in the BK parking lot after eating, the parts of her he'd put in his mouth, the parts of him she'd put in hers.

"You must really miss him," says Tammy, reaching back, opening her fist, and then taking Evan's hand into her own.

❦

THEY FUCK ONCE OR TWICE, Evan and Tammy, just after she breaks up with Victor and just before she hooks up with the painter she will marry after school is through. It's even fun, except for when she fakes her orgasms, which she seems to do for his benefit, maybe because she wants him to feel like some part of him isn't broken, which she knows is a lie, which is why she fucks him in the first place: in the hopes that her lips will heal him, or her cunt, or maybe even just the look in her eyes as she looks up at him and sighs his name.

But he is broken, all of him. It is the fourth of October, a year since Dad's brain seized up for the last time, like the game is seizing up now, and he is still balling his eyes out on a daily basis. Evan takes the cartridge out and blows into the end of it, trying to get the dust out, wiping at his leaky eyes as he does. Tomorrow is his birthday. Maybe he'll buy a new game, assuming he can find a place that still sells them for this old junker, now that there's not only the Super version to contend with, but the N64 as well. Maybe he'll ask Tammy to come over again. After all, things with the painter can't be that serious, not yet. And it is his birthday, after all.

He slips the cartridge back into the N.E.S., pushes it down and into place, and then hits the power button. They are back in business. He grabs the notebook. He blows his nose.

۞

HE AND HIS mother celebrate at the Friendly's up the road, just over the New Hampshire border. She orders a hamburger, plain, well-done — the only way she'll eat it. He gets the patty melt, for comparison's sake. It is good, delicious even, but he hates every bite. Just like Mom to take him some place that ruins a memory of Dad. She was going to leave him and she's still pissed off that she never got the chance.

"How's school?" Mom asks.

He says nothing, stabs a French fry into his pool of ketchup instead.

"Have a favorite class yet?"

Damn, he thinks. *The fries are better, too.*

"Met any girls?" she asks.

"One," he says. "She slept with me because she felt sorry for me. I don't think she feels sorry anymore. Or, well, maybe she is sorry still, just for different reasons now."

His mother nods along, sprinkling her fries with salt. She has never enjoyed his candor, believes he has a disorder of some sort that keeps him from keeping his mouth shut when he should. She brought him to a doctor once, to have him tested, but his father swept in at the last minute and took him out for ice cream instead. Dad had black raspberry, Evan orange sherbet.

"What did you want to get for a present?" she asks, handing him the card he knows is filled with one hundred and eighty dollars in cash, ten bucks for every year of his life.

He shrugs, opens the card. He stuffs the wad of tens into his pocket without counting it, without really looking at it at all. "I was thinking of visiting Dad's grave," he says.

"No," she says. "It's your birthday. That is too morbid, even for you."

He shrugs, soaks up the last of the ketchup with the last of his fries.

"There isn't anything you want?"

He shakes his head. She drives him back to his dorm. When he gets out, she forgets to hug him. She doesn't realize, it seems, until he's almost at his door. Then she hurries herself across the grass, her heels sinking into the muddy lawn on every other step. He stands still while she wraps her arms around him, lets her do what she thinks needs to be done.

THE CAB from the college to his hometown costs him more than he'd imagined it would, but there is still plenty left over for the sandwiches and the ride back. When the thought strikes him that he could have asked Victor, he brushes it aside, telling himself that good old V is still mad about Evan and Tammy, even though he knows full well that Victor hasn't thought about Tammy since they broke up and has, in fact, moved on to the Asian girl who lives upstairs, a computer exec's daughter who loves buying him breakfast only slightly less than she seems to enjoy waking the whole goddamned house with her harpy's wails at two in the morning.

Evan has the cabbie drop him in Drum Hill, at the Burger King. He buys a pair of Italian chicken sandwiches — they're just back in season, while supplies last — and then he walks across town with them under his arm, to keep them warm.

It's dusk when he gets there and there's an old man by the supply shed, a ring of keys twirling around his index finger. Evan waves at him, then walks up the hill, toward the back of the cemetery.

He sets one of the sandwiches atop Dad's grave, then cops a squat on the grass in front, opens the notebook, and begins to run down the numbers. He pauses for a bite now and then, but doesn't really eat until he's caught Dad up on the game.

"The cartridge is crapping out on me at least twice a day now," he says. "I was thinking..."

But saying it, even to a hunk of granite, is harder than thinking it. Asking for permission, even when there's no one left to grant it —

Evan cries. He tries to stopper the tears by dabbing at his eyes with the only thing he has, the sandwich wrapper, but all he manages to do is smear melted cheese and cooling tomato sauce across his cheeks.

"I was going to buy something new," he tells his father's tombstone. "But I had to ask you first. And now there's nothing left, so it doesn't matter anyway."

Evan stands, runs away. He doesn't answer when the man with the keys asks, "What's that on your face?"

❦

IT ISN'T until he's back in his dorm room that he realizes he left the notebook behind. He empties his pockets onto his desk to see if there's enough, but there's barely enough to get across town, let alone across the state. And then, what about getting back?

He flips on the TV. Another season is complete, ready for him to document it. He slams his fist down on the game console and the TV screen goes black. The game's load screen flickers back for a second, then blinks dark again. Flickers, then goes dark.

Evan hits the N.E.S. again and the flickering stops. From the console's cartridge slot pops something small and copper. It lands on the desk, heads up, Mister Lincoln in profile.

"So that's where you were," says Evan, picking up the penny. "So, that's where."

He crosses his fingers as he hits the reset button, hopeful, ready to start over. The load screen comes up, stays constant. Evan does not reach for paper or a pencil. He reaches for the controller. Then, he plays.

NO, I AM

I find him at his desk in the night, the glow of his computer screen like a halo around his head. He's turned from it, staring at the painting of ships in the harbor that he thinks his muse, looking for someone waiting on the waves to tell him a story.

Waiting, like I am.

When I tell him I'm scared, a stuffed animal in my arms, he jumps in his chair and shouts "Jesus!" before he can stop himself. He turns around and asks me what I'm doing up — what am I thinking? — and as I look down toward my feet I can see his chest heave in panic. I watch him huff and puff, and I'm so sure that he's going to blow my house in that I start to cry.

"Shit," he says. "Shit, shit, shit." And then he gathers me up in his arms like the burden that I am.

I weep softly into his t-shirt as he runs his fingers through the tangled hair I forgot to brush before bed. As I close my eyes, I think of the photo of us from the day I was born: my tiny body pressed against his chest as he holds me and smiles for the camera. He held his cheek against the top of my soft head while I searched with my open mouth for the only true thing I'd yet found in this cold, cold world. He held his cheek there like he's holding it there now, and, as the story goes, he told me he was sorry. A preemptive apology, Mom told me, because that was his thing, had always been his thing, because maybe he knew how often he'd need to be forgiven, because maybe he knew what was broken inside of him better than we ever could, better than he'd ever let us know.

"I'm sorry," I tell him now, my tiny voice muffled by his barrel chest and his beating heart.

"No, I'm sorry," he says, kissing my forehead once and then again.

"No," I say, "I am."

WHERE IT HURTS

Janet learned to hate her feet on the first day of second grade, when she wore flip-flops to school and Lizbeth English teased her about her big toe, how much bigger it was than the others. Lizbeth teased her about the hair on her legs too, and her *My Little Pony* t-shirt, which was *so* last year, but for Janet it all came back to the toe. If she hadn't worn the flip-flops, Lizbeth wouldn't have found her opening and would have picked on Mary Russel instead, whose legs were just as hairy and who was wearing a *Dukes of Hazzard* jacket besides, which wasn't so much last year as it was last decade.

This is what Janet is thinking about as little Audrey Hamel walks away from her Genevieve, arms crossed, tears in her eyes, to stand alone at the bus stop. This is the picture Janet wishes she could paint for her daughter right now to wipe that smug look off her face.

But Janet can't show Genevieve a thing, because the bus is here and all there is time for is the last second hug that Gen never forgets to give her mother, the last minute kiss on the belly that is meant for the baby inside.

Audrey Hamel is smiling by the time she boards the bus,

laughing at some joke told by the obese woman who drives it. But Janet can spot a smile for show from a mile away. It is her job to spot the fakers, to teach them to be real.

"It is not about acting," she tells her students, "but reacting."

Some glaze over; others reach instinctively for the notebooks she has told them will not be allowed in her class. Three take in the lesson without words, without the exaggerated nods their classmates offer up. Those three, they already know. They will be the most fun.

She sends them home with two assignments. They are to pick a Shakespearean sonnet and they are to memorize both parts of a scene from *Godot*, a scene none of them will ever understand — except perhaps for the bright three — but then, that's the point. She wants them to be able to regurgitate the words on command. Then, they'll spend the rest of the semester shaping their verbal vomit into any number of forms. They'll make comedies of it, tragedies, and everything in between.

"The words alone mean nothing," she tells them. "It is what you do with them that counts."

When she visits the playwriting class that afternoon, across the lawn in the second of the college's two classroom buildings, she does not say such things, though she believes with all her heart that they are true. Instead, she tells the budding playwrights that, without their words, an actor has nothing, can do nothing. There is one student who takes both classes. He does not call her on her contradiction. But he does write it down.

She meets her husband at the snack bar before heading home to get Gen off the bus. Tom is an admissions counselor, a salesman for the school, and his three-button suit is as much a part of him as his impeccable smile. He does not so much play the part as he inhabits the role. And when Janet tells him about the scene with Audrey Hamel that morning, he is quick to move into his second favorite sales pitch: the case for Genevieve's innocence.

"Gen is a critic," he says. "Her mind is incisive. She calls it like she sees it, and the only problem is that most kids her age aren't ready for her particular brand of honesty."

Janet sips at her Coke — no longer Diet, because of the baby — then nibbles at the taco salad she knows she will not finish, that she knows will end up in the trash alongside half-eaten hamburgers, on top of French fries made soggy by sodas dumped for having too much ice. Her stomach churns at the image, even as she tries to turn off this terrible visual mind of hers, all the more visual since the pregnancy.

"Did she hit the kid?" Tom asks.

"No," says Janet.

"Then it's not really bullying, is it? Teasing maybe, but — "

"It doesn't matter what you call it," she says. "I don't want Gen acting like that."

"You don't want Gen acting like herself?"

That's right, she thinks, but does not say. You're damned right I don't.

Tom has a point about Gen, though. Janet can't deny that. While Tom is at work at that night, the girls watch *The Transformers: The Movie*, and it is Gen who points out why Janet can tolerate it and not any of the episodes of the cartoon series. Tom has been introducing those to Gen little by little, since she fell in love with the movie during tech week for the college's summer show, when there were seven daddy-daughter date nights in a row, when Janet wasn't around to say "No" — her favorite word in the English language, according to both Gen and Tom.

"You like the movie," Gen says, "because there are conse-quences." It's a word she's surely heard, with a harsh-grading professor for a mother, but not one Janet knows her to under-stand. "This time, when Optimus and Megatron fight, one of them dies."

Death, the weakest of a storyteller's options when trying to make something matter, but the one the novice reader or listener or viewer is most likely to comprehend.

"Also," says Gen, pointing to the pink robot on screen now, "there's a girl."

"Who is barely anything but a damsel in distress," says Janet.

"What about how she saves Daniel?"

"The little boy?"

Gen nods.

"Well, that's something," says Janet. "But why is it that the most heroic thing she does is maternal in nature?"

"Maternal?" says Gen.

"Motherly," says Janet.

Gen turns her attention back to the television set. "You don't like being a mom very much, do you, Mom?"

Janet does not, in fact, enjoy parenting anywhere near as much as Tom does, or as much as the Hallmark cards she keeps in her hope chest told her she would when she opened them and the gifts she was showered with all those years ago. It's a lot of work, the job of being a mother, and there are questions on the exam her daughter administers daily that were never covered in the books she studied, and studied, and studied again. Janet looks at her stomach, at the bulge of an elbow (or, perhaps, a knee) as the baby makes itself comfortable. At times, during her weaker moments, she's not sure why she's doing it again, except perhaps as part of a dare from Tom: "Do it better next time, if you think you've sucked so much this time around." She looks past the belly, down at her toes, recalls Lizbeth English and her perfect pigtails.

Incisive. Was that what you called it, that ability to find the place that hurt the most, to drive the knife in there, and to keep on twisting?

"I'm sorry," Gen says, remote in her hand, the TV muted. "Are you mad at me, Mommy?"

Janet says nothing. She unmutes the TV, gathers Gen up in her arms, and then snuggles with her on the couch. The robot that looks like a hot rod, he picks up the so-called Matrix of Leadership, and the next time he transforms he is no longer a hot rod but an RV with flames on its hood.

Janet says: "Do you think the movie means to imply that growing up, that taking on responsibility, automatically makes you lame?"

Gen says nothing, though Janet is convinced it's not because she doesn't have an answer. Gen wants to say something. Janet can tell by the way she chews on her lower lip. That Gen holds herself back — that's proof of something. But Janet's not sure what, not yet.

❦

THE NEXT TIME her acting class meets, she selects two of the brightest kids and pairs them up. She tells them they are to play ancient, bitter rivals, about to fight to the death. They have a grudging respect for one another. But, more than that, they know what will hurt the other most.

"Did you ever read the Bible?" says the first, excitement in her voice, hope.

"The Bible?" says the second one, waving a dismissive hand in the air as he stalks away from the first. "I must've taken a look at it," he says, yawning.

Their choices are over-the-top, obvious. But they are also strong. By the time they reach the end, the first on her knees, about to be strangled by the second as she prattles on about the trouble with one gospel saying that a thief was saved at the crucifixion when the others say nothing of the sort, the rest of the class is ready to applaud. Their hands clasped together, waiting to break free and clap.

"Who believes him?" says the second, wrapping his hands around the first's neck.

"Everybody," says the first, in between choked breaths. "It's the only version they know."

The first actor dies, collapses in a heap. The second falls back onto his ass, exhausted at the effort. The class applauds, stands, applauds some more.

"Why did it work?" she asks them.

"Because he killed her," says the class smart-ass, an art student in paint-stained overalls who's taking the course as an elective.

"Consequences," she tells them. "She wanted one thing and he wanted another. The end result: consequences."

The third of the bright trio, the one who sat out this time around, she raises her hand.

"Yes," says Janet.

"Wouldn't it have worked even better if she put up more of a fight? Or if she was even capable of doing so?"

Janet smiles at her. "Yes," she says, embarrassed she didn't get there first, but proud the student didn't let the conversation get any further without the point being made. "Indeed, consequences are important. The stakes must be high. But we arrive at the consequences of great scenes only when the unstoppable force meets an immovable object."

She looks down at the sweaty, panting pair of actors at her feet. "Let's try that again, shall we?"

❧

JANET AND GEN sit in the car the next morning, the first time this year it's been too cold to stand outside for the bus.

"What do you think of Audrey?" Janet asks Gen, as the other girl's mother drops her at the corner and then, seeing that other parents are there to keep watch, makes the turn onto the main drag.

"We are not friends," says Gen, pouting, a bit of a snip and a snap in her voice.

"Why not?" says Janet, but before Gen answers she is out the door and laying into Audrey again.

Janet watches for a moment before leaving her car, hopes they will work it out, but when Gen grabs Audrey by the arm to keep her from running away, Janet knows it is time to intercede.

All of the other parents, all of the other children, they stay in their cars.

Janet grabs a girl with each hand and holds them apart, at arm's length. They are flailing at each other as Janet separates them, but Gen, respecting Janet's belly and what it represents, stops right away. Audrey, less aware or maybe just less concerned, swings one final haymaker of a slap in Gen's direction, but misses, her hand making a hard *thwack* as it connects with Janet's midsection.

Janet steps back, more shocked than hurt. The baby kicks, then kicks again. Janet lets go of the girls, puts her hands to her stomach, and feels a third kick, a reassurance from the creature within that it is OK, if a bit pissed off.

Not as pissed off as Gen, though, who is on top of Audrey now, punching Audrey in the head with closed fists.

"My baby," she shouts. "You hit my baby, you meanie. You stupid, mean dummy."

One of the fathers leaps out of his car. He tries to pull Gen off, but Gen's got a hold of Audrey's hair, two fistfuls of it, and she's not letting go.

As Janet unfreezes and moves to help the father, prying Gen's hands free, she hears more doors opening and closing, the pitter patter of feet rushing toward the bus, its screechy brakes announcing its arrival. Then, she hears another mom say, from under her breath, "Kid had it coming, but still."

WHEN JANET STOPS by Audrey's house later that night, Audrey's mother does not make a fuss. She asks about the baby, which is unharmed, according to the gyno, then says, "It's not the first time. Won't be the last. It's fine."

Janet wants to ask what she means by that, but Audrey is crying about the TV now, begging her mother to change the station, and Mrs. Hamel excuses herself, closes the door.

At home, Gen is working on her line for the school musical, one sentence from a children's story she will recite, in addition to the songs she and her classmates will sing. When Janet comes in, Tom looks up from his book of crosswords and Gen asks if they can watch *Transformers* now.

"Given what happened this morning," says Janet. "I'd say no."

Gen moves her lips, as if to speak, but abandons her protest, goes back to reciting her line. Tom looks at Janet, arching an eyebrow, then nodding at Gen in some sort of plea for leniency, a silent "Lighten up." As she goes to the kitchen, Janet wonders why he always gets to play the good cop.

Over dinner, Janet asks the question again — "Why did you pick on Audrey?" — but Gen hasn't responded to it all day, so Janet isn't expecting much.

Gen sets down her fork. Having eaten her requisite seven bites of pork chop, one for every year of her life, it is likely her next words will be a request to leave the table. But, it turns out, they are not.

Instead, she says, "I'm trying to teach her. Like Kup and Hot Rod in the movie. She says things she shouldn't. She does things she shouldn't. I tell her to stop." Gen shakes her head, sighs. "And then she cries," says Gen.

"Gen," says Janet, "it is not your place to — "

Tom grunts, raises his eyebrow again. Janet thinks, for a moment, about ripping the damned thing off and shoving it up his ass.

She does not.

She is about to continue when Gen says, "Audrey makes other people cry. I don't think that's OK."

"If it's not OK when she does it," says Janet, "what makes it OK when you do?"

Gen says nothing, then asks to be excused.

Once Gen is gone, Tom stands up and begins to collect the dirty dishes.

"You want to say something to me?" Janet asks him.

He says nothing as he moves to the kitchen sink, as he rolls up his sleeves and gets to work.

Janet leans against the counter, watches as he scrubs. "The dishwasher broken again?"

"No," he says, "sometimes I just like to do things the old-fashioned way."

"Is that my problem?" says Janet.

"I don't know what your problem is," he says.

Janet plucks the towel from off of the oven's handle, grabs a dish from the strainer, and begins to dry.

It isn't until the dishes are done that Tom speaks again, that he says, "You're always trying to teach her something. A lesson."

"And I'm teaching her the wrong things?" says Janet, as she makes her way out of the kitchen, as she flicks the light off before he's even made it out of there.

"Not the wrong things," he says.

"What would you teach her?" says Janet.

He leans against the doorway between kitchen and dining room and he sighs. "I wouldn't teach her anything," he says. "I'm her parent, not her professor. My job — our job — is to listen, to empathize, not to lecture, not to preach."

She shakes her head at him. "If I'm this bad at this, why did you get me pregnant again? Huh?"

He goes around her, around the whole dining room table, so as not to even have to touch her, to move her out of the way.

"No answer?" she says. "You've got nothing."

"I didn't mean to," he says, before he heads upstairs. "I sure as hell didn't mean to."

⚜

IN CLASS, as a form of mid-term evaluation, she has them all play the same scene in turn: one is a bully, the other is trying to get the bully to cry, to show him the error of his ways. It is up to them who plays Vladimir, who plays Estragon.

It is the two weakest actors who nail it, a pair of roommates who have shown up late all semester, the smell of pot in their unwashed hair, the last remnants of their morning high lingering in their bloodshot eyes. They still can't do their sonnets from memory and barely get through *Godot*, despite how many times they've done it, how many times they've seen it done.

They fought over a guy, earlier in the year, one of them spreading lies about the other's promiscuity to ruin her chances. And so, what they do is not an act. When the first calls the second an imbecile, the second feels it. It is not just an interpretation made in the brain, but a punch felt in the gut.

She feels it, and then, as Janet has taught her, she reacts. She does as she was told, not just by her teacher, but by instinct as well.

"Well, what of it?" she spits. "And why not?"

⚜

IT IS A TUESDAY, the Tuesday before Thanksgiving. Gen is in the car with Tom, skipping this last day before the break to head north early. Janet has been left behind. She has a final lesson to teach before she can join them. It is a short drive to the school, but the temperature is climbing — oh, New England! — and she decides to walk instead.

Audrey is at the bus stop, alone for the moment. Janet checks her watch, realizes this moment won't last long.

"Hi," says Audrey. "I'm sorry about your belly."

"It's OK," says Janet, buttoning her coat as a semi whips by on the main drag, its trailer of logs leaving behind a scent of cedar, of life where there is none left, on this road where the last of the fallen leaves were swept away weeks ago.

Audrey fixes her stare in the direction the bus will come from. She nudges the toe of her boot into the frostbitten earth, breaks a clump of it free.

"Listen," says Janet, "Audrey, do you mind if I ask you a question?"

Audrey shrugs, looks at her feet, at the bit of earth between them. She starts to pick the dirt free from the grass.

"What does Genevieve say to you to make you cry?"

"Nothing," says Audrey. "I don't cry."

"Oh," says Janet, kicking at the dirt herself now, digging her own hole.

"She says I'm mean," says Audrey, "and that no one will ever like me if I don't start being nice."

"Do you think that's true?" says Janet.

"It's fine," says Audrey, sounding like her mother, that word — *fine* — making Janet's heart ache.

"I don't care if people like me," says Audrey, walking away.

Janet means to say more, but the other children are coming, and it's time to get going anyway, or she'll be late.

She starts walking toward the college, but stumbles on the holes she and Audrey made, tumbling to the ground, her gloved hands all that stand between her belly and another trip to the doctor's.

"You OK?" asks the dad who rescued her two weeks before, on that day Gen and Audrey fought. He offers a hand to help her right herself.

"I'm fine," she says, not thinking about the word until it's already out of her mouth. She brushes herself off and gets back to walking, even though taking the car would be the wiser choice at this point. Her toe is aching, her big toe. That monstrosity. It will ache the whole way there, and the whole way back, and all the way through class, but she shouts back to the father that she is fine, just fine.

PARAMETERS

The robot sat upon my grandfather's stone wall, one clawed hand chiseling away at the rock while the other hurled pebbles at a nearby elm. It had been sitting there since the day Gramps trudged into the forest with his shotgun some eight years back, never to be seen again. Through rain and snow, it sat there. Through fallen leaves that choked its joints and creeping vines that clutched its spindly legs together with a child's determination and ferocity. I passed it every day on my way to and from the bus stop for school, sometimes stopping to sit a moment and sometimes not. It didn't seem to mind if I took a pebble or two and joined in its game, but whenever I tried to make friends, asking about the point of its exercise, the only thing it would say was "Two birds."

The day of my driving test, the last day I might make my walk until I had children of my own, I took to our long driveway early. When I reached the end of it, I sat with my back to the robot, watching cars zip along the two-lane country highway that was our road. I was nervous, and something about the robot soothed me. I don't know whether it was the pungent smell of lightly burning lubricant or the subtle scraping of one metal plate against another, but there was something comforting about this old machine. In the land of confusion that we call high school — Will Mr. Catmull realize I haven't read *Beowulf* today? Will Natasha smile at me when she finds the note I shoved into the slats of her locker? — in this world of variables, the robot was my constant.

"Why didn't Gramps ever give you a name?" I asked aloud.

"Two birds," it said, winding up and chucking another pebble at the tree.

I shook my head and smiled, casting my gaze at the ground. Horse-chestnuts had begun to fall from the tree that stood at the corner of our yard and the neighbor's, many of the spiked brown shells still intact. But a few of them had been cracked open, either by animals or by cars like the one that sped by at that very moment.

With hair whipping across my face, I plucked a fistful of nuts from the dirt and spun on the spot to face the robot's elm. But just as I was about to heave one at my target, the robot threw its arm out in front of me.

"Stone," it said.

"What?" I asked.

"Grandfather said stone. One stone, two birds."

And then it went back to its chore.

"Wait!" I said. "What?"

"Play with you, he said. Keep you away until he can go. One stone, two birds."

I wrapped my hands around the robot's throwing arm and squeezed, the metal cold against my fingers on this October morning. It would not look at me. It kept trying to throw the stone.

"If gun fires," it said, "Grandfather's pain ends. If Grandfather's pain ends, Grandchild's burden lifts. One stone," it said. "Two birds."

"Wait," I said, squeezing harder, as if that might make a difference. "No," I said. "That's not how it works."

"Grandfather says," it said, standing, something cracking down below, though whether it was its legs or the vines that bound them I couldn't be sure.

I hung from its outstretched arm as it rose to its full height. It tried one last time to throw the stone despite the encumbrance that was me, but then, realizing the futility of the exercise, it reached down with its chiseling hand and grabbed a stone with that.

I watched it hurl the rock at the elm, watched the rock hurtle toward the nest that was nestled into the V where the tree cleaved in two, and then watched in horror as the nest tumbled toward the ground, eggs falling from it as it fell.

The robot turned its face to me finally and smiled.

A PUN IN THE PUNCHLINE

We met in the conference room at the back of the building, a small room with a table that reminded us of a surfboard. It was the only room free at that time; inexplicably, every other room on campus was booked from 4 to 6 on Tuesdays. The professor had looked, had gone through each of the college's ten buildings, across campuses on either side of the river that cleaved our town in twain. He had searched, room by room, and had found nothing. Not even the abandoned dance studio was free, its broken mirrors and out-of-tune piano fodder for this semester's course in advanced art therapy. There was only the surfboard room at the back of the student center. And so, that is where we met. That is where we beat on, boats against the current, borne back ceaselessly into a past where our school gave two shits about us and our stories.

It had been six weeks since Cain had missed his deadline and we'd had to punish him, but we'd been coming back to the topic of our having gone too far with increasing regularity. Sure, we were honor-bound to defend the syllabus' rules and regulations — it was a contract, after all — but even the professor seemed to be feeling a bit of remorse. While he waited for us to file in each week, he kept his gaze fixed on the twenty-sided die and weathered D&D manual that had decided Cain's fate. And when the workshop reached an impasse that seventh week, when silence took the room, the professor, before saying a word to get us back on track, he ran his fingers over the foxed, dog-eared pages of the old tome and let out a sigh.

And so it was that we were each assigned a piece of Cain to bring back for week eight.

Jules collected the right shoulder and arm from beneath the newsstand at Pickett Square. Azar retrieved the left leg from the floorboards of the crumbling Episcopalian church at Philbrick Circle. Me, I dug up the torso and left arm from where we'd stashed it beneath the flower bed outside the provost's window. Corey found out where the right leg had run off to, but never told us. And the professor, he collected the head from atop the science building's dome, skedaddling out of there just as the seniors were getting ready to reassemble the car of the dean of institutional advancement as part of their annual prank.

"Where did the dean find the money for a Beemer?" the professor wondered. We would find out at an all-campus meeting the following fall, when that dean rode off into the sunset with his embezzled fortune and we all got shipped off to other schools to finish our degrees. But I'm getting ahead of myself.

Heads turned and noses were pinched as we strolled through the student center that eighth week, each of us with our heavy, malodorous burden. We drew the shades, we laid out the pieces of our comrade on the surfboard table, and we looked to the professor for guidance on what to do next.

"Well, it's such an exquisite corpse," he told us, looking at me, "that I think you should decide what happens next."

THE PRICE

He delivered the bodies to the riverbank at sunrise, when the opposite shore was aflame in the light of a new day. And as he waited for the ferryman to arrive, he lit himself a cigarette and inhaled deeply the poison he hoped would soon make him a passenger on his cart instead of the driver. With the butt pressed between his lips, he fumbled in his pockets for the six coins he'd need. Presently, the palming and patting and clutching grew faster, more furious. The first five had been easy enough to find, but by the time he caught sight of the ferryman dragging her skiff ashore, the sixth coin was still missing.

He kept his eyes on the damp hem of the ferryman's robes until the woman had drawn to a stop and rasped, "They are not ready."

Eyes still focused on the robes, on the sand that had clung there, he said, "I'm one coin short."

"Which stays then?"

He looked now at the ferryman, at the pallid, gaunt face she kept hidden beneath her hood, and he pleaded for mercy.

The ferryman plucked the cigarette from his mouth and pressed it between her own lips, taking a long, slow drag.

"They all must go," he said. "I am paid to make sure of it."

She handed him back the cigarette, stained at one end by the paint upon her lips. "If you are paid," she said, "should I not be?"

He pat himself down again. "I'm sorry," he said. "I swear I had it."

She took hold of his arms, stilling him with both the strength of her grip and with the iciness of it. "We may yet reach a bargain," she said.

"My soul in place of the final coin," he guessed, shrugging off her grasp. "That is no bargain."

"But I see it in your eyes," she said. "I tasted it on that poisoned teat from which you suck. And besides," she said, taking gentle hold of his hands again, "it is not the whole of you that I seek. It is just a piece."

"And which piece might that be?" he asked.

She lowered her hood, squinting in the bright morning light as she did. And then she undid the clasp at her neck and pulled off the robes entirely, holding them out for him to take.

He could not help but gawk at the slight form before him, the waif in the white dress who looked positively diminished without her robes.

"For how long?" he asked, running the coarse fabric of the robes through his fingers, noticing only now the places on her pale skin that had been rubbed raw by her accoutrements.

She smiled at him, and in that smile he saw the truth of it.

"Until I am owed," he said. It was not a question.

He watched her dance across the sand as he pulled the robes onto himself. Then he carried the bodies one by one to the skiff and set them inside. And it was only then, as he stepped back to give the cart one last check, one last goodbye, that he saw it laying in the sand, nestled into the print of one of his boots: the final coin.

He picked it up, held it above his head, and shouted for the woman who'd worn the robes, but she was gone. Long gone.

VISITATION

Rain splattered through the screen on her window, and though I pled with her to shut it, she would not budge. "I am disinclined to acquiesce," she said, smiling, quoting the film she'd been watching on her tablet in bed.

"I'll take that away," I told her.

"But I brushed my teeth," she said, showing them to me, the whole crooked lot. "And I'm in my pajamas," she said, pinching the fabric between her thumb and forefinger and pulling it away from her chest.

"It might get wet," I said, pointing at the window.

With a frown, she jammed a finger against the screen to pause the movie, then handed it over. A skeletal monkey grimaced at me from the frozen frame before I clicked the tablet off. I wondered suddenly if my daughter might choose a capuchin for her familiar. Or would it be the chicken she swiped across the road on her tablet because dice and tabletops made no sense to her?

"Now," I said, "will you please let me close the — "

"But what if they come?" she said, waving a hand at the rain. "I can already hear the footsteps."

She had given up on the jolly old demigods and cotton-tailed minor deities I'd told her (much to the chagrin of her mother) were nothing more than the servants of God Money, but the sprites and faeries of her storybooks — those she still believed in.

"All I hear is the downpour," I said, clutching the window, ready to close it.

"The downpour means they're close," she said. "They're almost here."

I looked at her then, at the brown eyes her mother had bequeathed her, at the sadness there, the longing for something I couldn't take away, and it hurt me to think of all I had robbed her of. I shifted focus, stared at an earring instead, the tiny amethyst stud her mother had bought her on the day she'd gotten her ears pierced, jewelry I'd refused to let her wear for a month out of frustration.

I sighed and stood. Then I pulled on the chain of her bedside lamp.

"What about my kiss?" she said.

I leaned down and pecked her temple with my lips, feeling a smile wrinkle her face.

"No souvenirs this time," is what I said as I left the room.

THE FIRST TIME IT HAPPENED, she toddled into my bedroom on a Sunday morning clutching a teddy bear to her chest, one that I'd never seen before. And after I asked her mother at drop-off that afternoon if she'd been splurging again, earning me the kind of dressing down I hadn't faced since The Dissolution, I decided it was a gift from my mother. But the truth was that I'd never asked and made sure, and now I was too afraid of what the answer might be.

The second time was a few years later. I was sitting in bed, three chapters into a freshly cracked mystery, when I realized she hadn't yet climbed into my bed with a brown bag of comics plucked from one of my long boxes. I swept into her room in a panic, nearly tripping on the long snake of the belt I never bothered to tie round my robe. But, as sure as I was in that moment that I'd lost her, there she was: in her bed, crumbs everywhere, a thick slab of gingerbread in her hands. There was icing tucked between her fingers, smeared all across her face, and caked into her blonde hair. And though I asked and asked where she got it as I stood outside the shower, all I got in the way of an answer was a sheepish grin as she poked her head out from behind the curtain to ask me for an extra towel.

Would tonight be the third time, I wondered. And what gift would she bring back if it was?

I stood outside her door and listened to her breathe, waiting for the rhythm to change. But it was hard to hear her over the cacophony of the rain, so I closed my eyes to focus. Soon, though, I couldn't hear her at all, and I rounded the corner with haste.

But she was still there. She shivered, tugged at her blankets, and rolled so that her back was to the window.

I sat on the floor, leaned into the wall, and stood watch. And when her breathing grew shallow enough that I could no longer see her chest rising and falling, I held a hand to her belly until her body pushed me away.

I drifted off to sleep.

And then I was awake, my head aching from where I'd slumped against her dresser. I rubbed a hand across my face, then looked to my daughter's bed to see if she was awake, to see if I'd have to apologize for being a creep.

She was gone.

The bed was empty, the covers pushed aside, and all that was left of her was a smear of blood on the sheets. I could only look for a second before seeking solace from the open window. But there was no absolution to be found there. The rain had stopped. There would be no gift this time.

Or so I thought, until the toilet flushed just beyond the wall.

I rushed to the bathroom door, listened to the rattle of pills in a bottle, the running of a faucet and its cessation. Then I heard a groan. A groan and the patter of bare feet across cold linoleum. I stepped back as the door opened.

"Dad?" she said, holding a hand to the place where I supposed it ached.

Though I knew I shouldn't have, I gathered her into my arms and held her to me.

"Sorry about the sheets," she mumbled into my shoulder.

"Do I need to run to the store?" I said, letting her go.

She shook her head. "Mom's had me packing stuff for six months, just in case."

I nodded, gave her a smile, and watched her trudge back toward her room. I couldn't help thinking, as I listened to her strip the bed down, as I listened to the bundle of sheets hit the wall and her body hit the mattress, if I had lost her after all.

An hour later, she knocked at my door with a brown paper bag clutched against her chest.

"What you got?" I asked.

She pulled the first issue from the bag. On the cover, a capuchin sat atop the shoulder of a man in a straight jacket. "I know it's for mature readers," she said. "But..."

I smiled at the hand I'd been dealt, at the card she was playing, and I said, "Okay."

She smiled now, too. "Can I sit with you?" she asked.

"That's not weird?" I said.

She rolled her eyes and climbed up onto my bed, sitting down beside me. "It's only weird if you make it weird, Dad."

I bent to kiss her forehead, hoping that I hadn't, knowing that someday that I would.

"Read," she said, pointing at my book.

And so, we did.

THE REST OF THE RITUAL

They are rolling the car toward the river. Through the yellowing fields I once taught them to sow, they push the jalopy with heave after coordinated heave. Sweat has stuck their shirts to their backs. Or, well, it's stuck the shirts of the two who bothered to wear shirts. The third, he's bare-chested in the noon-day sun, his shoulders already redder than the lobsters their wives are stewing in the pot back at the house. When they break, he's got one hand working the crusted-up snot out of his nose and the other down the front his pants, scratching at the spot where his drenched briefs have begun to chafe against his spindly legs. He asks, just as he did when they were boys and he was sucking down Cokes through a straw in the back seat, "Are we there yet?"

There is the hill, the downward slope that will send their monstrous burden over the cliff and into the churning rapids below. There is where they will say goodbye to what's left of me on this earth, the body their wives have dressed in a suit that hasn't fit for years and laid across the back seat.

"We're laying Pa to rest," says the oldest. "For Pete's sake, quit your pissing and moaning."

"And get your fingers out your nose," says the youngest.

The bare-chested boy, he removes his hands from their hiding places and wipes them across the seat of his pants. "I just don't understand why we have to light it on fire."

"We light it on fire," says the oldest, "because that's what our people do."

"Our people?"

The youngest slaps him upside the head. "Vikings, you idiot."

The bare-chested boy shakes his now-sore noggin. "Don't they do that with an arrow, or something? Once it's out to sea like?"

"Like we're gonna trust you with a bow and arrow," says the oldest.

When they reach the hill, once they sense the vehicle beginning to move of its own accord — with a little help from Granny Gravity, o'course — they put blocks in front of the near-flat tires and grab a rusted red canister of gasoline from the front seat. The oldest does the honors, anointing my trusty steed with the holy water of the rambling man. The youngest thumbs through a grease-stained Bible he pulls from his back pocket while my middle boy stands idly by, rubbing at his red shoulders and wincing, rubbing and wincing.

"Can I light it?" he asks his brothers.

They look at him, then each other. Him, then each other. I reckon they're wondering if he'll miss while tossing the match, if he'll set the field ablaze instead of the car.

"I thought you didn't understand," says the oldest.

"You learned me up," says the bare-chested boy.

The oldest rolls his eyes, then nods at the youngest.

The youngest pulls a book of matches from his other back pocket, untangling it from the lint and loose thread that's wrapped itself all around the book. Then he tosses the matches to his brother.

While the bare-chested boy works out how to strike a match proper in the wind rolling in off the snow-capped mountains and down across our tiny valley, my youngest boy begins his recitation, orating a psalm. My oldest ducks his head, tries not to think about the thermometer his wife showed him before he left their bedroom, her encouragement to hurry back because "It's all in the timing." He knows they've been out here too long, but he's also sure I deserve everything they're giving me.

How I wish I were solid for one more second, so I could punch him in the arm and tell him to get back to doing what needs to be done, to forget about what's gone — and who, o'course — and let his brothers tend to the rest of the ritual. But I ain't, and I can't.

The youngest nods at the bare-chested boy, who finally has a match aflame, his hand cupped around it to shield it from the wind. The bare-chested boy tosses it and finds his mark. And then, as flames begin to lick across the hood, my oldest removes the blocks and together they give the car one last shove.

It rolls toward the cliff and they chase after it, chasing after it like boys running down butterflies when their papa's trying to learn them what matters. Then the car jumps over the edge and begins its descent. They watch it, hoping for the explosion, hoping they've done it right and they'll send their daddy soaring up to heaven before his body finds its way to hell. And they're still watching when the fire takes me wherever I'm bound to go. I try to judge by their faces where that is, but only one of them is smiling, and it ain't the sharpest tool in my shed.

BOOKS & LETTERS

When he sees her pulled from the register to reshelf things, he finds himself a dark corner in the stacks in which to hide. It doesn't matter which corner — yesterday it was between Weight Loss and Human Sexuality, today it is amidst the tomes of Religion and Philosophy — but he must hide. He cannot see her.

Three days ago, he mailed the letter to her house. He didn't know where her locker was at school, after all, so how else was he supposed to do it? And for three days now, he has waited, waited for her to find him and give him an answer. As he stands there, thumbing through *The Celestine Prophecy*, he imagines he could make it easier for her, but he's scared he would drop a book on her foot again. For, like, the fifth time. She always tells him that it doesn't hurt, but she's stopped wearing shoes with open toes now, so he knows what's what.

"*Hem, hem,*" comes a voice from behind him.

He slaps the book shut and jams it rudely into the first empty spot he sees.

A squat woman dressed all in pink steps toward him.

"I'm on my break," he tells her.

"For how much longer?" she asks, nodding discreetly toward the cafe that fills out the back of the bookstore. There is a line forming there, he sees.

Just as he is about to respond, the girl rounds the corner with her cart and they lock eyes.

The woman in pink looks from boy to girl, from girl to boy, and gives her head the smallest shake. She walks away.

"I'm on my break," he tells the girl.

"Okay," she says.

"It's almost over."

"Right," she says, ducking her head and nodding. And then, when a lock of hair falls down from her neat bun, she tucks it behind her ear, looks up at him one last time, and nods.

He stands there until she's shelved the book in her hand, until she's taken the cart and pushed past him onto whatever comes next. It is only when he hears the *Hem, hem* one more time that he remembers his role and dashes off to play it.

⚜

AT SCHOOL THE NEXT MORNING, when he opens his locker, the letter is there, wedged into the slats at the top; he's surprised he didn't notice the edge of it jutting out before he opened the door.

He holds it for a second, the letter, as his classmates crowd around him, nudging their way toward their own lockers in the cramped hallway. But he pays them no mind, doesn't respond to their elbows or their glares. He needs to take it in.

The envelope has been opened neatly, cut at the top by a letter opener he imagines she stole from her father's office. And his letter is there too, but there's a smaller piece of paper, a purple one, wrapped around it. And she's scrawled a note upon it.

There's someone else now, reads the first line. *I'm so sorry*.

But it's the second that gets him, the words that appear just above her looping signature: *The books hurt less than this does.*

He tosses his own letter back into his locker, then folds hers into a neat square. He stuffs it into his wallet, hides it in a corner so dark that even he will forget where it is.

Except that he will always know it is there. Always.

DOGS

What Marla remembers the most is the way the middle of the suitcase lurched upward as the kid slammed it atop the hood of her truck, the way the middle bulged so big at that moment that she thought the fabric of the thing would tear and send the horror within soaring. There was the thud of course, and the sound of the kid's Chuck Taylors slapping against the pavement during the escape, but nothing was as vivid in Marla's mind as the lurch, as the dog's body, bound within the suitcase, bouncing into the air one last time.

This is the story she thinks of at the Legion while nursing a Gansett and listening to an ex-cop's yarn about discovering a dead dog in the bed of a missing Pittsburgh kid some years back. The kid — a wealthy writing student at the local college — it turned out that he done the deed before skipping town.

"Two in the chest," says the cop, "while pulling a B&E. His accomplice? Get this: it was his professor."

"Get outta here," says Marla with mock-enthusiasm.

"I am not shitting you," says the cop. "It was all hushed up by the college, o'course. Probably why you never heard of it."

"That," says Marla, "or the fact that I ain't never been to Pittsburgh."

"Nah," says the cop. "If that'd made the news, it'd be all over. National story, I'm telling you." And then, after a healthy pull from his Coors, the cop adds, "Fucking academics."

"Fucking A," says Marla.

MORE THAN ANYTHING, Marla wishes she could forget. She wishes she could forget shit that doesn't matter, like the name of the guitar-playing punk who sang about the United States of Whatever — Liam Lynch, she remembers, with a wrinkle of her forehead, a twinge in her temples — and she wishes she could forget about the shit that does. That did.

Back in the day, before she left the wilds of Maine for college in the big city, she owned this Australian shepherd, and there's this picture of him she has to shake every time she gets called out to deal with some supposedly rabid stray that's harassing the country clubbers up the hill. The picture is of she and her mutt by the fence of the family farm, the sows he was charged with wrangling blurry in the background, her arms around his neck. There is mud matted in his fur and caked on her windbreaker. A day later, he will run into traffic to chase down a runaway piglet and he will be crushed beneath the wheels of a Jeep Wrangler plowing down their country road. But now, in the picture, in her memory, he is alive and well. His tongue is loose, his one blue eye focused on the camera as he poses, his chest puffed out and proud. In her head, he never dies.

And she wishes he would.

STILL, she keeps one dog around at all times. Two, if she's fostering some mongrel she can't bear to see put down. And now, as she stands on the lawn behind the Legion, staring across the pond at an empty beach in the twilight, trying to shake the cop's story out of her head before it finds a dusty corner to call its own — even now there is a dog beside her. She doesn't know its name — there's no tag — and doesn't know where it came from, but Marla, sucker for punishment, doesn't shoo him off and tell him to go home. She lets him stay there beside her, lets his drooping belly imprint itself on her brain, lets her brain imagine where the scar on his left ear came from, whether he was overfed before the incident or only in the days since.

But she does better this time, better with the part that always makes her want to forget. She doesn't let her mind wander to the natural conclusion, to nature's conclusion for this poor pooch. Instead, she sends herself backward and sees a puppy chasing butterflies in a field...

...or pigs...

...or a little girl who won't ever want to forget.

VENTRICLE

I've forgotten how to hold myself together, so that the cyclone twisting around my heart is tearing one ventricle from the other and casting off the weaker half of me into the gunmetal sky, like the house Aunt Em and Uncle Henry used to own (before the market crashed).

Crashed, crash, crashing — I am crashing now into a land of make believe named after the second drawer of a filing cabinet. A filing cabinet!

As I search the prairie for the bloody half-organ that's been taken from me, I lament my compulsion to understand how things work. I long to be able to read a sentence again for the pure joy of it, never wondering how the writer got to the snow over Ireland or why it was general and not merely widespread.

I am not the first to find my heart. A straw man has torn himself down from his cross, a woodsman in rusted tin armor has dragged his way out of the forest, and a lion cowers in the shadows of an old oak, lying in wait amongst the poppies growing in its shade, hoping the others will go away.

They stand aside when they see me, though. Me and the hole in my chest. Yes, they stand back and let me pluck the ruined thing from its place in the corn. They do not protest in word or in deed. For, while they may be wretches, they are not thieves.

I fit the thing back into my chest and sew the loose flap of flesh to my collarbone with a ribbon I pull from my hair. Then, I wave goodbye to the menagerie and I make my way back toward the house.

"Don't you w-worry," the lion asks me, "about another twister? About it happening again."

"It happens every day," I tell him. "One day it will kill me, but not today. Not today."

FORKS

After the funeral and the burial and the celebration of life where distant relations and overreaching parishioners drank his liquor cabinet dry, Andre found himself across the kitchen table from a girl whose index finger was buried deep in the cavern of her right nostril. She'd scrunched up her eyes and her nose, as if squeezing together the features of her face might make it easier to unearth the treasures inside her hollow head. Andre's stomach churned at the sight, but he said nothing, even though he supposed it was now his place to do so.

The girl belonged to the wife that Andre had just put in the ground, a leftover from a marriage gone by, and she was now Andre's by law. At least until she bled and curved out and he could pass her off to someone else. Maybe even get a dowry out of it, if he could get her to stop picking her goddamned nose.

"Not very ladylike," he said, picking at his teeth with his thumb.

"It's right there," she said through gritted teeth, still digging.

Andre reached into the suit coat he'd hung over the back of his chair and produced a hankie. He held it across the table for her to take.

"What am I supposed to do with that?" she asked.

"Blow your nose," he said.

"Never learned how," she said, finally calling her finger back from the hunt.

"Never learned?" he said.

"Never," she said, wiping her finger along the bodice of her dress, mucus smearing across the new black fabric.

"You put your nose into it and blow," he explained, miming the action.

"That's awful," she said.

"And what you're doing isn't?"

The girl's eyebrows ticked up upward ever so slightly as her painted lips trembled.

"What?" said Andre. "What did I say?"

"My mother," said the girl, a pair of tears chasing each other down her cheek. "My mother taught me to do it this way."

"I never saw her," Andre began, but before he could finish, the girl stood up sharply from the table, her chair toppling backwards onto the floor, and she said:

"No, you didn't."

ANDRE MET the woman and her daughter on the third of July, down the center of town, where he took townsfolk up in his hot air balloon for a quarter a pop. They were the first in line, wanting to get a ride in before claiming their spot along the sidewalk for the parade the next day, and they were all smiles as they climbed aboard.

When Andre asked "What're your names, my pretty ladies?" he was told by the young girl that they were Carla and Carlene respectively.

"Respectively?" he said, with a smile of his own.

Carlene, the daughter, she pointed at the gap along the right side of his grin, and she asked her mother what happened to the nice man's teeth.

"Lost them," he said, closing the basket's door and latching it. "Lost them in the war."

Carla, the mother, set a gloved hand upon his bare forearm and gave him a little squeeze. "Oh, you brave soul," she said.

He smiled again as he adjusted the flame and took them into the air. "No bravery required to lose a couple of teeth," he said. "Just a German boot in the wrong place at the wrong time."

She tilted her head a touch and raised the corners of her lips in a weak attempt at a grin, then said something about his modesty as they lurched upward—a rockier beginning to their ride than Andre had hoped for. But when she stumbled into him, her chest pressed against his, her gloved hand still on his arm, he did not feel sorry.

Though he did say, "My apologies" as he steadied her, as he held out a hand to steady her daughter as well.

"My apologies" — it was what he said to her in the dark of her bedroom that night, as well, when he finished before she could.

She laughed loudly, then quickly covered her mouth as she looked to the door to see if her daughter had been woken.

The starched sheets clung to his back as he rolled off the top of her, came with him in a twisted mess and left her naked in the moonlight.

"You," she whispered, "are the first man to ever say that to me."

"A French girl taught me manners," he said, as Carla rolled onto her side and ran a hand along the contours of his chest.

"What else did she teach you?" said Carla. "Something to make it up to her?"

Andre blushed.

Carla slapped his chest so hard it stung, so hard that the sound echoed through the room. She looked to the door again, held still as she waited for a light to come on in the hall.

"What was that for?" asked Andre.

"You can't just blush," said Carla. "You have to tell me."

Instead, he showed her.

"DID YOU LOVE MY MOTHER?" Carlene asked him.

It was the morning after the funeral and he was spooning sugar atop his apparently tasteless corn flakes in the hopes of appeasing her sweet tooth. The marriage had been young when catastrophe struck, the relationship not much more mature. There had been barely two months in which to learn what these women ate, how they spent their day. Barely two months to learn — or *not*, as the case might be — of their nasty habits, the affectations he would have to adjust to in this house where he had lived according to routines established by his own mother a lifetime ago.

He stepped away from her, toward the refrigerator, to gather up the milk and to compose an answer for his lips and for his face. He had appreciated Carla, had been fond of her, of waking to the sight of her pretty face half buried in a pillow on his bed, but had he loved her? He'd been working on it, but that wasn't what the child wanted to hear.

Lost in thought, he opened the ice box instead of the fridge, and it was only the blast of cold air that broke him of his reverie.

Inside, there was nothing but a wrapped-up piece of wedding cake, something he'd been convinced to save for their first anniversary. As he stared through the cellophane at the thick icing piled atop the white cake, his stomach grumbled in hunger.

"You can't have that," said Carlene. "It hasn't been a year yet."

He turned on her and snapped, "And who's going to eat it when that day comes, huh?"

Her lip quivered as she waited for what he'd say next. What he'd do. But when he said nothing, when he did nothing but slam the ice box door shut, she stood from the table and ran out, leaving the dry corn flakes behind. The last of his cereal sat uneaten in her bowl, sugar dusted across the top like the layer of dust upon his mantle. The mantle that Carla had taken to cleaning since moving in, on Saturday mornings just like this one.

He sat at the table and picked a single cornflake from the bowl, shaking off what sugar he could. Then he put it into his mouth and let it soften on his tongue, thinking of how little time there had been to change things, and of how much had changed in spite of all that.

⚜

THE FEVER HAD COME on fast, taking hold of Carla's body just as the summer loosened its grip on their small town. She must've picked it up at the diner, she told him as she slipped into a night-gown at midday and took to bed. Couple of regulars'd had the sniffles, and that must've been it.

But then the coughing began. It shook her body and echoed through the house. Blood and phlegm filled the steel bowl he ferried back and forth from her side to the toilet. And yet, as scary as those days were, the silence that followed was more frightening than anything that had come before.

One morning, after having dozed off in the armchair he'd dragged from the parlor to the foot of the bed, he woke to find Carlene sitting at her mother's side, dabbing at Carla's forehead with a damp cloth.

"What are you doing?" he asked the girl as he wiped the sleep from his eyes.

"Making her comfortable," said Carlene.

"You shouldn't be in here," he said. "You might catch whatever's caught your mother."

"You're in here," said Carlene. "What if it catches you first?"

"I have a strong constitution," said Andre.

Carlene scoffed. "That's what my father said before he died."

"I was a prisoner," he told her then. "And the things those Krauts did to me — if I could survive those, then a little fever isn't going to hurt me."

"It's not little," said Carlene, dipping her cloth into a bowl of water that looked too much like a bowl of filth for Andre's taste.

Carlene looked back over her shoulder at him. "How'd you escape?" she asked.

"We didn't," he said. "They were about to get rid of us when another army, friendly to ours, came rolling in."

"You were rescued," said Carlene.

"Yes," said Andre.

"The way you rescued my mother and me," she said, wiping again at her mother's forehead.

"I suppose," he said. "I suppose that's true."

She stared at her mother then as she said, "You're better at *being* rescued."

⚜

IN THE NIGHT, Andre woke at the sound of Carlene's feet padding down the hall. He turned to wake Carla, to ask her to check on her daughter, but all that was there to nudge was a pillow that had already lost the shape of the woman's head.

Andre hoisted himself up then, swinging his legs over the side of the bed. He sat for a second and closed his eyes again, listening to the sound of his lungs expanding and contracting, a trick he'd learned in the hole he'd been kept in during the war. He'd learned it to keep the sound of his empty stomach from infecting his every waking moment, but it did the trick now, too. There was something in the corner of his eye that wasn't sleep, and he didn't want more of it to come spilling forth when he wiped it away.

Up he got, once the moment passed, shuffling down the

hallway himself, breathing deeply again as his knees locked themselves up and voiced their crackling concerns.

Then, suddenly, a light flashed on in the kitchen, a bright slice of yellow cutting through the dark for but a moment before it was gone again.

Andre quickened his pace.

When he rounded the corner, realizing all he'd brought with him to defend himself and Carlene were his fists, he put up his dukes anyway. Just in case. But he needn't have. There was no intruder, no abductor nor villain of any sort. There was only Carlene, seated at the kitchen table, the slice of cake plated before her.

"I'm hungry," she said, not looking at him. "There's nothing else left."

Andre pulled a chair out from under the table and took a seat, staying silent as he did. He remembered a moment with Carla, one of their few spats, where she'd told him over a burnt roast that the whole thing could have been avoided if only he'd shut up and listened.

"It's not my fault," said Carlene, her gaze still fixed on the frozen piece of cake. "You won't go to the grocer's. You won't buy us food."

It was the word *us* that brought forth the sniffle from his nose, an involuntary sound. He wondered if that would count against him.

"Are you crying?"

In his mind, he told her that he was coming down with something, but in the real world he held those words behind the prison of his teeth.

"I can't eat your tears," she said, sounding like she'd like to try.

Deciding that action was not the same as speech, Andre reached across the table and pulled the plate toward himself.

"You have to share," said Carlene, a quaver in her voice. "I'm starving."

Andre looked away from her for the first time since sitting down, focusing on the cellophane. Carla never did anything half-way, did she? It was wrapped up good and tight. His eyes squinted in the dim light creeping in from the street lamp outside, squinted as he searched for some corner to pull on. He spun the plate around once, then again, then once more before he found what he was looking for.

When the slice of cake was finally free, he slid it back across the table to Carlene. In his hand then, he balled up the cellophane, relishing in its crinkles and its crackles as he did.

"You'll need to let it thaw for a bit," he said as he stood. "I'll get a fork."

And now it was Carlene who said nothing, who sat silent in a room permeated by this unexpected kindness, as unexpected for him as it was for her. She said nothing until the drawer of silverware squeaked open. It was only then that she told him to grab two. Two forks instead of one.

RECEDING

The soldiers smoke their last cigarette on the last boat out, passing the shriveling thing amongst themselves. One of them, the one in the sunglasses, he hangs onto it for too long, sucks too much of the life out of it and leaves too much of himself behind when he finally passes it on.

"You might as well have laid one on me," his buddy tells him, rubbing the drool off with his thumb and forefinger, then flicking it at Sunglasses.

All of them look forward, these men, paying attention to the pal upfront with the camera who is there to make sure they go down in history. All of them look forward but one. He casts his glance backward at the fjord they're leaving behind, wondering if it would be wrong to say the fjord is retreating, wondering if that's what they're doing too. And, if that's what they're doing, why is everyone else smiling? The sea sprays up and back, white as the snow capping the now distant cliffs.

Receding. That's the word, he realizes. The fjord is receding.

As he is. As all of them are.

All of us, too.

ACKNOWLEDGEMENTS

"One Player or Two?" was first published in *Commonthought 2013*.

ABOUT THE AUTHOR

E. Christopher Clark is the author of the Stains of Time series, a family saga with a hint of magical realism and a whole lot of time travel. His other books include the short story collections *Out of the Woods* and *Under the World*, the novella *The Seven Wives of Silver*, and a collection of poems cheekily titled *Bad Poetry Night*. His short stories have been published in *Live Free or Ride: Tales of the Concord Coach*, *River Muse: Tales of Lowell & the Merrimack Valley*, and the University of Hawaii's *Vice-Versa*. A graduate of Lesley University's MFA in Creative Writing program, he lives in Massachusetts with his wife and daughters.

echristopherclark.com

facebook.com/eccbooks

x.com/eccbooks

instagram.com/eccbooks

goodreads.com/eccbooks

pinterest.com/eccbooks

amazon.com/E.-Christopher-Clark/e/B00H0G94T0

www.ingramcontent.com/pod-product-compliance
Lightning Source LLC
Chambersburg PA
CBHW021938170626
46807CB00007B/3168

*9 7 8 1 9 5 2 0 4 4 0 8 3 *